Break the Glass

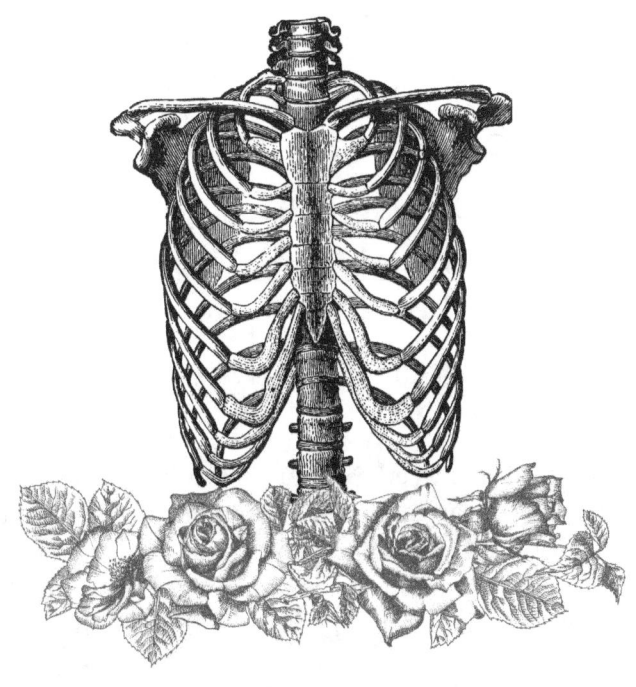

Jack Whitney

This one is for Alexis.

Thank you for constantly inspiring and hyping me up to take things to the next level.

Warnings

Break the Glass is a paranormal erotica novella with a
dominant Bloody Mary inspired main character,
the "this is pure fucking smut" trope, and some horror
elements.

Because of the darker elements and erotic nature of the acts
within, it is not recommended for persons under 18 years of
age.

The following are the darker topics to be aware
of within this novella:
Demon, demon hunter, ghosts, summoning, mild horror, and
mentions of past assault.

This book features erotic and BDSM elements and actions
between two consenting adults. Please do not attempt these
actions without proper education, safe words,
communication, and aftercare.
There are a lot of resources out there to consult so that you
and your partner have a pleasant experience, and this is not
one of those guides.

These are the BDSM and erotic elements
to be aware of:
Femme Dom, blood play, spitting, edging, blowjobs, shadow
bondage and pegging, choking, voyeurism, spanking,
praise/degradation, and brief use of a crop.

This is a **work of fiction**,
and is not meant to be any sort of manual to impact play,
summoning, or any other situations you may find within
these few pages.
Please read and enjoy a bit of fun spooky smut.

Happy Spooky Season, ravens.

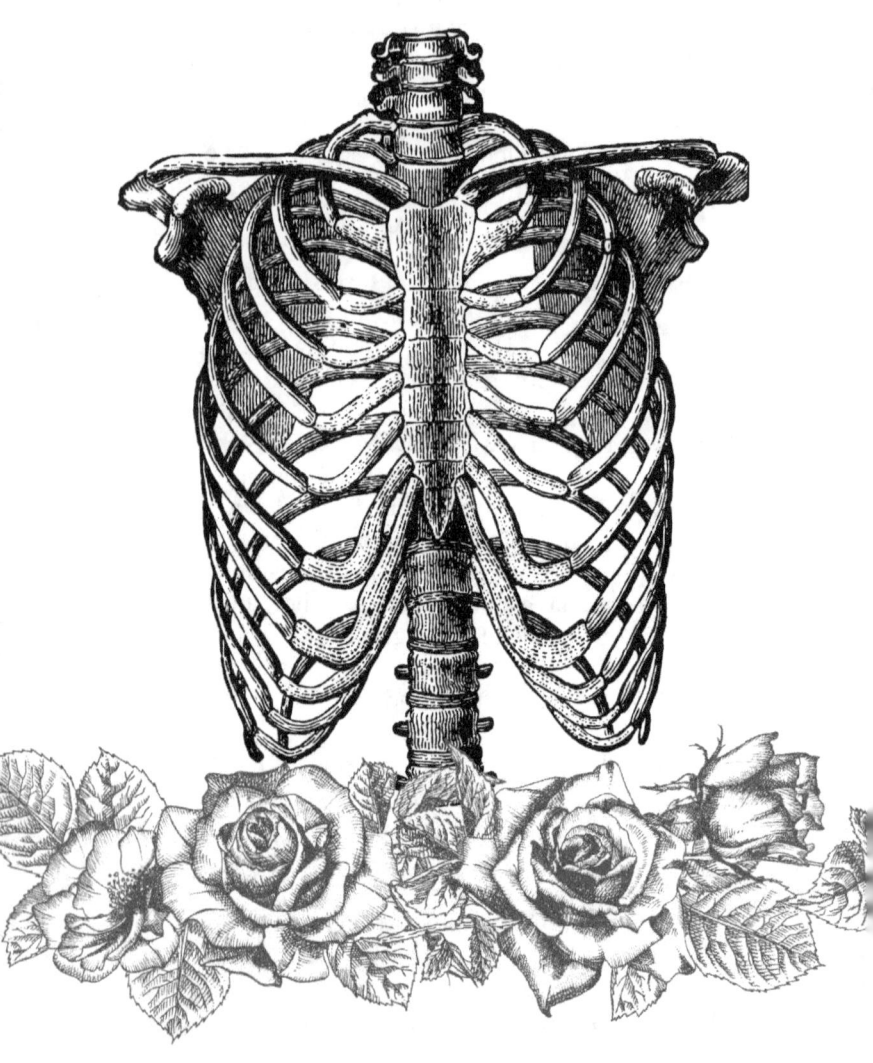

Chapter One
Damon

THE cold chill of late October wrapped around me as I strode past the wrought iron gates and onto the mansion's grounds. Dying grass and broken limbs cracked beneath my black boots, scaring away any rodents and sending the crows fluttering into the air.

I'd searched years for what lurked inside this mansion. Years of standing in front of mirror after mirror and screaming her name, only to come up short each time. It had to be the right mirror, so the other demons had said. The right time of year. And only at the stroke of midnight.

This was Mary's curse for all that she'd done in her life.

Mary. The demon dubbed 'Scarlet Mary' who had taken down person after person on her way to becoming a tyrant. Mary, the demon that supposedly took unwilling men back into the mirror after seducing them. She'd once been free to any mirror, but after murdering and taking so many bodies back to her realm, she was caught and trapped within this one.

I'd often wondered why she'd not been killed that day.

A few stones crumbled beneath my feet as I stepped across the pebbled pavers that were now overgrown with dying weeds. The mansion had last been occupied forty-seven years prior by a family who thought the mirror they'd bought would be the perfect centerpiece in the library. A book in their collection had revealed what truly lay inside that reflection, and it had been one of the children who had dared to set Mary free for a ravenous night.

Though, she'd left the young ones alone and only feasted on the parents.

Mary was forced back into her mirror at sunrise. I learned a few daredevils and spirited teens had summoned her over the years, thinking her existence was a hoax, and it was their disappearances that led me here to the mansion.

Cobwebs lingered over the wrought iron raven knocker and in every crease of the grand double-doors. I tried the oval doorknob—unlocked—and then pushed on the door.

It screeched open, and with its noise, crows flew

off the roof over the curved window to my left.

An ornate staircase greeted me upon entering. Leaves and dust scattered the dark floor, more cobwebs covering the sconces and grand chandelier high above me. I looked down at the makeshift map on a napkin that the last demon had drawn out, showing me where the library was, before then heading up the stairs, my flashlight being the only guide I had.

The smell of the mansion was the same smell I'd grown accustomed to over the years. It smelled of decay—not only of rotten leaves and debris but also of the loss of life. Something else pricked the air here, however. There was an iron tang in the stagnant air. Blood, I realized. Only Mary would use such a scent to warn those of her presence.

With a left at the top of the stairs, I headed down a long hall. Typical oil paintings and unlit lanterns lined the walls. I slowed to shine my light over a few framed photos on antique dressers. The last family who had lived there had left the photos behind, although the paintings on the walls were much older.

At the end of this hall was a spiral staircase. My map bore an X atop this, marking my final destination. I examined the iron stairs first, shining my light up through the ceiling to the next floor. The iron smell was more pungent here, the air cooler.

Every step creaked beneath my boots; the footholds rattled with the weight. I half expected it to come crashing down atop me, but it held, and I ascended to the next level.

It opened up to a foyer of sorts—another grand chandelier hanging high above, a small mirror over the dresser before me, and a set of gracious wooden doors to my right. I tossed my flashlight over and over in the air as I stared at the heavy doors, the iron rings where doorknobs should have been.

As heavy as the doors looked, they opened with ease. Chills rose on the back of my neck at the uncomfortable energy within the room.

It was a shame such a beautiful place had fallen under her spell. The library was massive. Books lined shelves on the story above, and two more spiral staircases in either corner on the opposite side of the room. A fireplace sat in the back, and in front of it was the largest desk I'd ever seen. Papers were strewn atop it like the person who had once worked at this desk had not anticipated their demise. Books were stacked on either side of it, all pulled from the extensive shelves on every wall. A thick layer of dust lined them. Tall candles sat in golden holders on the bookcases.

And there, in an alcove carved out of the room

with diamond-paned windows behind it, sat the tallest, most audacious mirror I'd ever laid my eyes upon.

This was the mirror of Scarlet Mary.

Nearly six feet tall, it was lined with thick, ornate golden trim—ravens and roses carved into it. The mirror itself seemed to have a depth to it, like it held its own world within the glass. Shadows lingered around me as I peered into its reflection. They seemed to swarm even in the places where my flashlight shone.

A whisper tickled my ear, cold air brushing my neck. In the reflection, I saw a slender hand with sharp fingernails tipped in black rake across my shoulder.

Help me, the shadow seemed to whisper. *Set me free.*

I flinched at the feeling of a tongue licking the shell of my ear.

Mary.

One glance around the room, and I knew it held everything I needed to summon her, contain her. I sat my flashlight on the desk and began to gather candlesticks and search the desk for chalk.

Within the hour, I had the room ready. I'd lit every candlestick I could find and placed them strategically around the binding circle I'd drawn on the floor. Satisfied with my work, I took off my jacket, rolled up the sleeves of my button-down, and pulled the oversized armchair from behind the desk, sitting it directly in front of the mirror, two feet from the edge of the circle. I liked dressing up for my more anticipated killings. It made them feel more like an event rather than my job. And Mary… well, Mary was a special case—my most anticipated kill.

I wondered what kind of fight she would give me… And I nearly smiled at all the possibilities.

I reached into my jacket and pulled out my cigar, lit it, and then sat down in the armchair. The first puff of smoke filled the air as I said the name that few dared to say, the name I'd screamed and shouted for so many times before.

But this time… this time, she was mine.

The mansion seemed to shudder the second time I spoke the words, spoke her name, but I held my ground, and I didn't look away from the mirror.

A shadow passed behind me, the long nails again brushing over my shoulder. I shifted and picked up the fire poker I'd sat beside my chair, and then laid it across my lap as I said the words one last time.

The air seemed to freeze.

A few of the candles blew out.

And in the distance, I heard a laugh.

The shadow behind me turned into the silhouette of a curvaceous woman. Long, wavy hair swept over her shoulder as she walked around the front of the chair. She blinked, and dull, red eyes glimmered back at me. I didn't move as her laughter faded, as she reached an arm out toward the mirror, and when she touched the glass, I knew the summoning had worked.

A long finger was the first thing to emerge. The sharp obsidian tip of her nail caused a ripple effect across the entire surface, distorting my reflection. A bare, pointed foot—toenails painted blood red—appeared next. Slowly, she stepped through, taking her time like she meant to scare whoever waited on the other side. And with every inch of her that emerged, I felt my hands tighten around the weapon in my lap. I didn't dare blink or look away, not even when my body resisted the shift it wanted to take as the siren demon appeared.

Fucking Mary.

I knew Mary would be desirous. I knew she would be beautiful, tempting, even unearthly in her seductions.

But Mary was desire itself.

Mary was clad in a midnight satin dress that hugged her pear-shaped frame, her hip dips, her voluptuous ass, and split low between her petite breasts. Her poison scarlet hair glimmered in the candlelight—long and wavy, the color of blood, the motion of the rippling sea.

Startling, though, were the scars riveted across her pale skin. Raised and raw and lethal... As though every time she'd been ensnared in circles like this one or beaten for being who and what she was when she was alive, was laid bare upon her flesh. The most concerning scar was the one that went over her left eye, splitting her cheek, eyelid, and brow. And the eye that stared back at me through that scar was a deep, nearly black shade of carmine.

Mary brought an arm across her chest and bit her sharp black nail between her teeth. Her long lashes hit her eyelids, showcasing the cat-eye points of her eye makeup, and a closed-lip smile rose on her darkly shaded lips, thus accentuating the curvature of her apple cheeks.

"Aren't you a pretty thing?" she cooed, swaying side to side. Her gaze devoured me, constricting my throat as I held the fire poker tighter in my suddenly sweating hand. Fuck, the way her eyes stared me down was new. I shifted slightly in my seat as I drew again from my cigar. I'd summoned and destroyed enough demons in my days to be wary of her games, her seductive looks, her taunts.

"Hello, Mary."

Her smile split, showing off perfectly white teeth behind those pouty lips. "Hello, demon hunter," she said, her voice like crushed black velvet—

smooth, seductive, and melting. "Do you usually dress up so much for your summonings?" she asked.

I blew out another plume of smoke. "Depends on the guest."

"Should I be honored?" she asked with a tilt of her head.

When I didn't answer, Mary simply took her nail from her lips and looked around at the circle she was ensnared within. Her tutting tongue clicked over the chilled air.

"Not very fair, hunter," she cooed. "You free out there, me trapped in here... What now? You have that pretty poker in your lap, will you try to kill me?"

I considered her slowly, letting her stew in that small circle for a few more moments before giving her the conversation she wanted.

Though she seemed to find the silence amusing.

"What's the matter, hunter?" she said in a teasing tone. "Am I not what you expected? Or perhaps—" Her eyes lingered on the front of my pants, tongue darting out and licking her bottom lip before she sucked it behind her teeth. The simple act made my jaw twitch.

"—perhaps I'm more woman than you expected, and it scares you," she continued.

"How do you know I'm a hunter?" I finally

asked.

She laughed, and the sound of it echoed in the small room. "Innocent beings don't look as you do when they summon me. They think they're going to be brave, though most of them run. And none are smart enough to bind me. It makes for an eventful night of play... So much blood." She licked the tip of her nail like blood had collected there at the memory, and her long lashes hit the back of her eyelids when she looked at me again.

"What's your name?" she asked.

I put the end of my cigar out on the chair, patting it when fire tried to ignite in its wake. "My name won't help you stay alive," I replied.

"I wasn't aware I had options." Her eyes raked over me again. "What do you want if not to kill me?"

Chapter Two
Mary

I loved the smell of this mansion.

So much history here, so much blood staining the walls, the tapestries, the furniture.

I'd drained an idiot college boy on the same chair my new hunter was lounging so handsomely in. And a handsome thing, he was.

His dark brown hair was swept back, a thick, yet short beard lined his jaw and wrapped over his top lip. Blue eyes cut through the darkness, the firelight reflecting off his golden skin. He looked so cross sitting there, his thick brows furrowed, causing the vein in his forehead to show itself. I'd never seen a man dressed up as he was—white button-down, black slacks, black boots. The dirt on his boots made me smile. So uncharacteristic of the put-together facade showing on the rest of him. Every time he tightened his large hands around the poker, the veins in his exposed forearms popped.

If I could get him to let me out...

Oh, the fun I could have with him.

How long had it been since I'd had a true challenge call my name? A demon hunter... I nearly laughed as I took a turn around the cute little circle he'd drawn.

"I want a lot of things," he replied to my previous question. "Right now—" he twirled something in his hand, and I took a step back as he revealed the ruby jewel and gold necklace in his palm. "Right now, I want to know the story behind this before I kill you."

I scoffed at his request. "Do you think that is enough to get me to beg for my life?"

Though just the sight of that thing made me squirm.

It had belonged to me when I was alive—given by my favored lover. It was the only possession of mine that I gave a damn about, and the thing had been my downfall.

A smile rose on his lips then, and I knew I'd made the mistake of letting him see that brief moment of vulnerability, but he didn't say anything. I hugged my arms around my chest.

"Give me your name, let me out of this circle, and I'll tell you whatever you want," I bargained, hating being confined to such a small space. It was as horrible as my mirror. My legs begged to stretch;

my body yearned for touch.

"What do you want with my name?" he asked.

"You know mine," I replied. "Why shouldn't I know the name of the hunter who will ultimately be my true demise?"

He considered me again, twisting that poker in his lap. "Damon," he finally said.

My lips twisted in satisfaction. Five minutes and he was already responding like the good little hunter I knew he was capable of becoming. "You must be scared, Damon," I said. "To want to hear a silly story instead of giving me a chance to run or killing me outright."

"I'm curious," he said.

"I'm sure you know what curiosity does to a person," I replied. "Especially ones daring enough to ask for stories from demons."

"It's a chance I'm willing to take," Damon said.

I stepped to the very edge of the circle, watching as he braced himself slightly. "Let me out," I said, my voice quieter. "I'll tell you everything your little heart desires."

"If I let you out—"

"If you let me out, I'd still be trapped to this mansion," I said. "To this mirror at sunrise…" My gaze flickered behind me to the monstrous gold mirror—my tomb, my prison. Doomed to walk behind that glass until summoned, or one day set free.

Wouldn't that be the dream?

"Be a good boy and let a girl play," I taunted him. "I know you want to. I can see it. Big man like yourself isn't afraid of a challenge, is he?"

"Get out of my head, demon," he snarled.

I moved a touch too far over the line on the floor. The tip of my nail burned as I drew back. He caught the suck of air I took, his satisfied, darkened gaze trickling over me in response.

I took another survey of him on the chair—the black pants and boots, the button-down shirt, the top of his chest exposed, that necklace between his fingers... The more I stared at him, the more appealing the thought of him touching me sounded. True, I did just want out to play, to run... I wanted to feel the air running through my hair, the wall behind my back, his hands on my wrists or pulling my hair just like I desired.

I wanted to tame this big man. I wanted the challenge of seeing him subdued just for me. I wanted to grant him freedom from this dominant prison he wore so well, to release him upon the world as my own.

"You know, you would be so much more adorable on your knees... *crawling* for me," I added. "All for a taste—" My hand moved over my hip and parted the slit of my dress before delving slowly between my thighs and touching my bare cunt.

His eyes glazed, jaw ticked, clearly annoyed at the arousal I could see pressing against the front of his pants. "You've been bound to that mirror too long if you think a demon hunter is going to crawl for you," he said.

I laughed coyly, rocking back on my heels and taking a single turn around my entrapment. "You forget who I am, what I've done, the hundreds of beings I've toyed with and taken back into my mirror to play. I can *smell* your desire."

Damon didn't bother stifling that need or readjusting in his seat. He twisted the fire poker again, flexing the veins in his thick forearms. I took a step forward, and the end of it whipped out in my direction, the tip nearly scratching my stomach. A warning that I welcomed.

I wrapped my hand around the iron and stroked it upward, delighting in the sparks that appeared when I dragged my nail back down its length.

Damon rose to his feet, not daring to look away from me. "You want to see me on my knees?" he asked, hovering a foot from the edge of the circle, teasing me with his proximity.

He choked the poker in his hand and moved it deliberately up my body, the sharp point snagging on my satin dress. My eyes fluttered as it stroked over my peaked nipple. He raised the weapon and pressed the tip harder into my skin.

A low groan left me as I looked at him and noticed how he was staring at my breast, at the way the iron tip threatened to break my skin.

A single drop of black blood dribbled down my flesh and over the iron, sizzling and boiling on the weapon's edge. I licked my lips as I watched his eyes follow that drop. His gaze slowly lifted to mine, and as though he were calculating his every breath, he moved to the very edge of my binding.

The energy within the circle bloomed with hatred, desire, and *rage*. This was his way of taunting me—to hover over the line that would burn me, tempting me to see how far I could go.

I loved it.

Finally, someone willing to play—a beautiful demon hunter at that.

I could mark him to my heart's desire.

I would let him think he was in charge here.

And after he'd had a taste…

I almost laughed at the thought of what he'd do for me then.

Mine.

Chapter Three
Damon

FOR the briefest second, I thought I'd made a mistake by stepping to the edge of her prison. Her eyes rolled up, those long lashes hitting her eyelids with devious intent, dark lips split—

Mary launched.

I caught her at arm's length by the throat, but she didn't lose the licentious smile on her lips.

"Ha," she panted, her tongue sticking out, eyes blazing in delight. Her body caved as she shifted in my grasp—a feral cat at the precipice of killing. She seemed to revel in this situation, at being at the end of her leash and taunting whatever part of me might be over the line.

"Teasing my boundaries, hunter?" she asked, her chest heaving. "I hope you're not looking for fear."

My thumb rubbed over her neck where her pulse should have been, only to find a hollow void. The black blood on her chest stared back at me when I let my gaze drop, and I realized I needed to see the rest of her, needed to feel the rest of her.

I'd taken a few demons like this in the past—let them think they'd won, enjoyed a night of chasing and rough sex. Usually, they were not smart enough to realize I'd never let them go.

But Mary... something told me Mary knew exactly what my plan was, and she didn't care, or perhaps meant to play me back. And something about that had my cock hardening.

"Take off your dress," I whispered.

A quiet chuckle left her when I released her, and she took one step back. Her finger lifted the spaghetti strap of her dress, letting it fall down her arm, then the same with the opposite side. My mouth dried at the sight of her now exposed breasts, the taut peaks of her pink nipples. The dress slouched at her belly button as she watched me take her in. A long scar dragged along her sternum, more raised scars across her pale skin, and I had the sudden desire to touch them.

"That's it," I said softly, watching her fingers run beneath the fabric again.

She pushed on the dress, causing the fabric to struggle to stay intact as she wiggled it over her broad hips. A ripping noise sounded, and I realized she'd torn the seams on either side to let it down. The satin garment fell into a puddle at her feet, and when she stepped out of it, I absentmindedly ran my tongue across my now dry lips at her fully exposed body.

What her flesh would feel like in my hands... how my fingers would dig into her skin, how she would move atop my cock, and how red she would be as I spanked her...

To put Mary on her knees before killing her would be the highlight of my career thus far.

She dragged her finger up the middle of her stomach, between her breasts, then cupped her soft tit and pinched her nipple—tight enough that she sucked in a breath. It was the taunt of that self-inflicted pain that prompted me to do what I did next.

I moved into her circle.

Mary's eyes widened slightly as I pressed one hand into my pocket and looked her over. The necklace I'd threatened her with lay in the very bottom of that pocket—within reach so I could use it were she to do anything drastic. Her head tilted back upon my approach, never losing sight of where my gaze lingered.

I stretched one hand down her flesh, memorizing the raise of each of her scars beneath the pad of my thumb.

"Like what you see, hunter?" she asked as chills rose on her skin. She was so soft... so supple. Every squeeze of my fingers caused her skin to redden around my handprint. The things I could do to her, how she would respond to me…

"You're just another demon to subdue," I said, a restriction in my voice that I hadn't anticipated.

The corner of her lip lifted. "Let me out," she whispered. "Subdue me without this binding like the dangerous demon hunter you are. Show me why I should fear you."

Provocation and danger laced her every word. A knot wove in my stomach at the insinuation, and I nearly reached back for the iron poker to brand her ass right then. Instead, I grabbed her by the face and launched her toward the very edge of her circle. Her hip and arm singed at the binding burning her flesh, and she hissed.

"You'll obey, demon," I growled as she wiggled in my grasp. "You'll obey because you value your miserable existence."

I threw her off, causing her to trip and land on the ground, her body curling up as she landed with a thud on the hardwood. Her hair covered her face when she lifted onto her palms, but it didn't muffle the sound of her laugh.

"Is that your best threat?" She whipped her hair out of her face and stared at me over her shoulder. "Or do you truly fear what I might do if you set me free?"

I walked toward her and wrapped a hand into her hair, pulling her back to her feet. She didn't resist, didn't whimper or whine. Her lips parted with a moan, and the sound of it sparked arousal in my gut. My balls tightened as her feet landed flat on the floor, her eyes blazing with desire.

"Throw me again and press those long fingers inside my cunt," she whispered, her bare breasts brushing my chest. "Find out just how wet you've made me with all your little warnings."

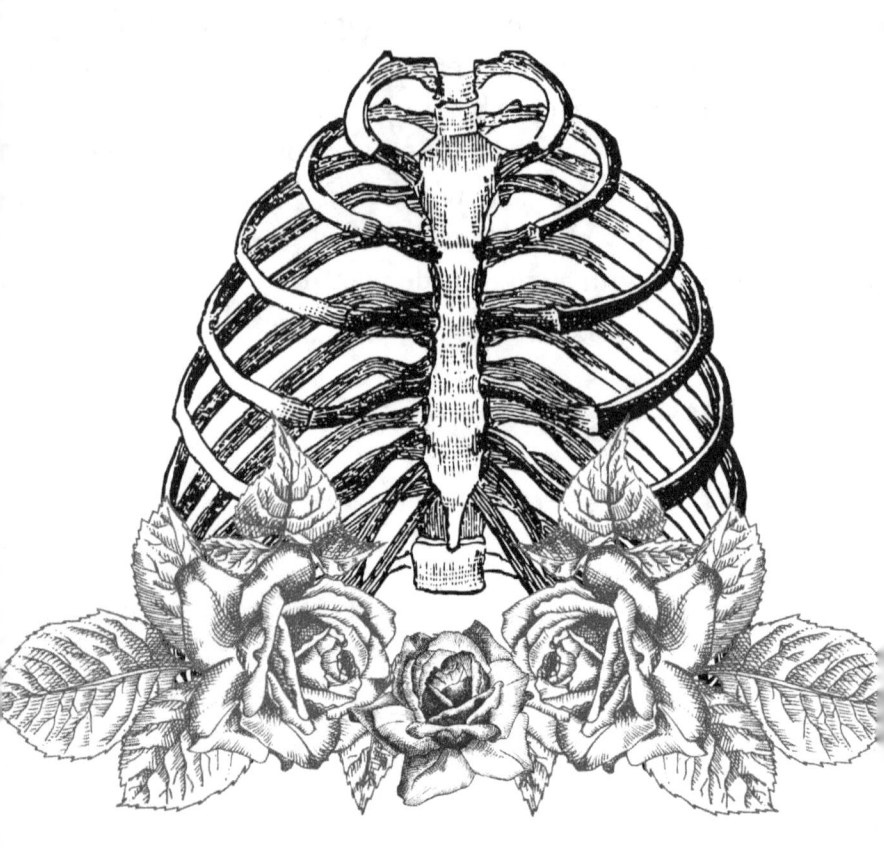

Chapter Four
Mary

DAMON'S grip loosened in my hair, allowing me to straighten and collect myself.

"You'll show me how well you obey first, demon," Damon said, his fingers running over my cheek to my jaw, the heated sensation causing hair to rise on my neck. He tilted my head back, thumb pressing hard into the soft spot beneath my chin. There was no play in the way he threatened me, and I stifled my laughter.

Very well. If this would get me further to him praying at my feet for more, I'd give him what he wanted. I could be patient—a virtue it seemed he lacked.

"Do you expect my worth to lie in how I suck your pretty cock?" I asked.

He released my neck gently, his chin dipping as he stood dominant over me. "It's a start," he replied.

The sinister laugh that left me felt close to the relief of orgasm. "My precious hunter…" I started around him, slowly stepping as I spoke, dragging my hands over his arms, back, and every rippling muscle beneath his button-down. He was a delicious specimen, an eager one—whether he knew it or not. I wanted to unravel my pretty new toy, but I'd start with unwrapping him first.

"There are so many other things I could do to you," I said, moving my hands around his waist. "So many other things you'd like more than just a foolish little blowjob."

With every word, I undid one of the buttons on his shirt, my nails scratching against his stern chest. He glanced toward his left shoulder as though he were keeping an eye on my movements, but he never stopped me.

I grabbed the fabric and gave a great tug, causing the rest of the shirt to rip as my sharpened nails scratched his skin. He jerked slightly but didn't move when I leaned up on my toes and bit the lobe of his ear.

"I could make you scream," I rasped, my hands crawling down and down his chest, his abs, to the belt of his pants. "I could make you come harder than you've ever dreamed." His leather belt was easy enough to undo, and he didn't move when I slowly untucked his shirt.

His abs flinched every time my nails tickled over or scratched him. Black hair curled beneath my fingers, leading down from the abs I wanted to lick and leave marks across, all the way past the waist of his pants.

The moment I began to move further, his hands snapped to mine, and he grabbed them so tightly that a sucking hiss sounded from behind my teeth. He turned around to face me, still impending my fingers, pushing them back like he meant to break them. And when he rounded over me, I bared my teeth in warning.

"Do that again," he said. "You're adorable when you imitate a cat."

I wriggled against his grip, but he pulled me in tighter, pushing our bodies flush until I was trapped. His breath breezed over my cheek, and just when his lips brushed mine, he shoved me backward.

I caught my balance this time and barely staggered. Damon held my gaze as he pulled the sleeves of his shirt off, fully revealing his broad chest, those muscled shoulders and arms, and the hair across his torso. He, too, bore scars along his skin—a long one on his left side, a few puckered ones on his left pectoral, scratches like he'd been mauled smattering that golden flesh... I wondered if these were scars from past demons he'd entrapped or something darker.

Damon's blue eyes darkened with the move of his head as he started undoing the button of his pants, the zipper, finally exposing his thick cock. It bobbed free, not fully erect yet, but making my mouth water regardless. Damon stroked his thick length, and I noted the pressure he used. The corner of my lip coiled upward at the pinch he took on his tip.

How long had it been since I'd had a participant so desirous toward pain like myself? The last few idiots had whimpered deliciously, but they'd been worthless in the end—another spraying of blood in the darkest corner of my mirror.

My lip sucked behind my teeth as I met Damon's gaze. His chin lifted smugly, and he gestured me forward with two fingers.

On my knees trapped in his little binding wasn't exactly the romantic setting I'd imagined, but until he let me out, this would do. I would make him forget the names of any others who said they could please him.

I moved to him, letting him have this one. He stroked himself again with his right hand, and with his left, he cupped my cheek. His thumb brushed my bottom lip as he whispered, "On your knees."

My nails dragged over his chest as I sank to one knee, followed by the other. His cock stiffened in front of me, and I stuck my tongue out to taste him. One lick, another, another… Damon moaned and scratched the top of my head in response. With every swirl and twist of my tongue, I took him further, digging my nails deeper into the backs of his thighs.

Every moan that left him made me drool a little more, made my pussy a little wetter. The pleasure I could rake out of him with just my mouth always brought me to the brink of coming myself. I loved the noises men made when they surrendered. I loved how their cocks tasted and when I choked or gagged on them. I loved edging those cocks until their owners begged and pleaded for release.

Damon's grip tightened in my hair when I tickled his balls and took him deeper, relaxing my throat. My cheeks hollowed when I dragged my mouth back to his tip and pinched his sack. I kissed the end of his cock and glanced up at him.

"How long can you hold out on me?" I asked, swirling my tongue on him. "Will you let me tell you when to come?"

"Fuck," he hissed, his palm massaging the back of my head.

He pushed me further, making me gag and causing saliva to drip from the corners of my lips. The taste of him sent me further and further into a frenzy. I moaned around his dick as I continued devouring and staring at him.

He kept glancing straight ahead, and I realized he was watching us in my mirror. Knowing how much of a show that was, I spread my knees wide and arched my back further, moving up and down every time I took him deeper.

"You like watching us, hunter?" I said, sneaking a glance at us in the mirror at my back.

But Damon grabbed my head and turned me back to him.

"Suck, demon," he commanded.

I resumed my ministrations, saliva dripping from the corners of my lips as he made me choke and held my head straight. I struggled for breath and gripped his legs in response to the hold, the pain, the rapture.

"Just like that… *fuck, yes*," he hissed.

When he loosened his grip, I slurped my spit as I withdrew. He was close… too close to coming.

I needed out.

So caught up in his pleasure, Damon didn't notice the shadows edging around every corner of the room. The circle restrained them from taking anything more than a few whispers of candlelight at a time. I glanced up at Damon, seeing his eyes rolling as I wrapped my lips around the tip of his cock, and I reached up to grasp the fabric of his pants.

"Let me out," I said, teasing him with my tongue between the words. "Break this circle… Fuck me like the bad girl I am."

He glanced down at me, pupils blown as he watched me deep throat him again. He twitched in my mouth, prompting me to suck him tighter upon withdrawing.

With a seizure of his fingers around my neck, he urged me off the floor. I obeyed and rose to my feet, letting his cock drag against my skin as I did. My nipples grazed his chest when I was once more standing. He tilted his head over me, his fingers squeezing my face.

"Did you like my cock in your mouth, demon?" he asked.

"Almost as much as you enjoyed my lips around it," I replied.

His grip loosened on my face, and he trailed his hand down my neck, my sternum—making sure to give my tit a squeeze before proceeding lower.

"I think you're a liar," he rasped. "And I think this wet cunt will enjoy my dick even more than your mouth did."

Yes.

"Touch me," I begged. "Taste me."

Let me out.

His fingers slipped between my thighs, and the moment he touched my pussy, he drew a deep breath. I was soaking, my cunt practically salivating at how close I was to being free. I let out a moan as he split two fingers on either side of my clit and began rubbing.

"You sound so nice when you beg," he said, his lips a breath from mine. "I bet you'll sound even more helpless when I tie you up to fuck you."

His promises did sound intriguing, and I even considered letting him have that one. But as he pinched my clit hard enough to make me squirm, I imagined him bound instead, and a gush of warmth spread in my core.

"Yes," I whispered.

"Scarlet Mary…" He shook his head with an almost victorious look in his eyes. "Pathetic little whore, just like the rest of your demon friends."

"Let me please you," I said. "Let me out so you can fuck me across that desk like the despicable demon I am. Make me scream before you take my miserable life."

"I will," he said, his nose dragging along my cheek. "Will you run?"

"Only if you want me to," I said, and I wasn't entirely lying. I reached between us to his erect cock and stroked it, eliciting a deep groan from him. "Please," I said.

He tilted my head back again, his knuckle under my chin. "Back on your knees," he said. "Put your hands behind your back."

I did, and he reached across the circle for the rope beside the chair.

As he bent over to tie my wrists together, I stared at the supple armchair, calculating every move I was about to make. The ropes scratched my skin when he tightened the knot, and when he stood over me again, I couldn't resist giving his cock another lick.

It was such a nice cock, after all.

"You're mine, demon," he told me.

Damon picked up his shirt, and the moment he began to wipe away some of the chalk on the floor, setting me free, my breaths shortened.

A small gap appeared in the circle. I felt it in my bones—the relief of freedom and inner chains breaking. My every muscle edged to the point of unrelenting restlessness. Damon stood again and dusted his hands off, his shoulders rolling back smugly.

"Stand," he ordered me.

I began to rock back and forth, a quiet chuckle sounding in the back of my throat, becoming louder and louder by the second. I was delirious at the feeling, at the person standing before me thinking I would obey and cower to his words. As though the threat of permanent death might frighten me.

My eyes rolled up to meet his, peering through my hair at the licentious man before me.

"*Sit.*"

Chapter Five
Mary

FLAMES evaporated.

Shadows swarmed.

Damon flew off the ground and slammed into the chair before he could get a word out. Within seconds, his hands were tied to the arms of the chair, ankles tied to the legs, leaving his own thighs spread, and his thick cock ready and waiting.

While he writhed and cursed, my shadows moved to me and began to undo the knot around my wrists. I summoned darkness over my bare body, creating a high neck lace lingerie bodysuit with the chest open, a split in the crotch, stockings up to my mid-thighs, and high heels that made me nearly as tall as him. A leather crop appeared in my grasp, and once I stood, I slapped the wide, heart-shaped end across my palm.

Damon yanked against the bindings. "Fucking whore—"

I sent a shadow to caress down his cheek. "Shh…" I caressed, pausing before him. "Silly hunter. Do you know what happens to bad boys who think they can tame me?" I asked.

"You're delusional," he spat.

My smirk widened with a low scoff. "So cute," I said as I dragged the crop teasingly down his throat. "Tell me to stop."

The fire in his eyes blazed. Arousal, hatred, and outright desire stared back at me. He didn't protest. A smile flicked on my lips, and I pushed over him, one knee on each side of his lap. I moved my entrance over the tip of his cock, but I didn't sink onto him, not even when he cursed my name under his breath.

I flipped my hair over to one side and leaned down, tickling his cheek with my nose as I whispered, "I know the kind of man you are. The kind that gets off on a woman's pleasure. The kind that looks at a wet pussy and salivates. You'll be my little dog, and I'll edge you until you can't help but scream my name." My hips rocked against his length, making him suck in another breath.

"You *crave* this, Damon…"

I straightened over him, shifting up so that my breasts touched his chin once more. He looked like he was going to taste me, but I moved away.

"Open your mouth."

Damon's eyes met mine as my finger brushed beneath his chin and tilted his head back. Slowly, I watched that stern hatred leave his gaze, and he dropped his jaw.

Warmth puddled in my core, so much so that I was surprised I was not dripping on his cock by how wet I became. Seeing that surrender, that trust in what I was about to offer him... I had not threatened to kill him, had not told him I would beat him senseless if he did not do as he was told.

I offered him freedom, and the hunter took it. It was sexier than anything I'd ever seen—anything I'd ever felt.

My hand wrapped around his cheeks, hollowing them out as I squeezed. "Stick out your tongue."

I delighted at seeing his tongue move, feeling his body shake, his knuckles paling against the armchair as he suffered beneath my shadows. And when his tongue was where I wanted it, I pushed higher on my knees and collected saliva from every corner of my mouth. It dripped in an elongated lead from my mouth and hovered over his tongue a moment before landing on its target. I released Damon's face, pleased with him as he swallowed.

Sitting back on his knees, I began to stroke that big cock of his between my hands, rewarding him for his behavior. "Now, tell me what you'll say when you've had enough," I asked in a sing-song voice.

Damon's jaw tightened, his chest heaving as he watched me. "Mercy," he whispered in a gravelly voice.

"Sorry, what was that?" I asked as I squeezed his cock, and a drop of precum dripped over my thumb.

"Mercy," he ground out.

I chuckled at the strain on his face and reached up to pat his bearded cheek. "Someone's been doing their research. What a *good boy*."

Chapter Six
Damon

SON of a fucking bitch.

I was used to being in charge—in both my professional life and my personal. But this...

She was right. I did enjoy pleasing my women, but I had not experienced this. A woman who knew exactly what she wanted, who would reprieve me of any show I might think I have to put on to please her. This was freedom and total unrestraint. I hated to admit how much I wanted to know what she would do to me, what she was already doing to me, what she'd want me to do to her.

Mary stood off my lap then, causing my abs to constrict with the vacancy of her warmth. Her broad hips and ass swayed as she moved back a few steps. The lingerie she'd summoned with her shadows had me salivating. After the way she'd sucked my dick, I was ready to taste her, feel her, touch her—had been prepared to turn her ass bright red as I fucked her across the desk.

Though, maybe she'd let me do that later.

The shadows… Why had I not anticipated them? Of all the stories of her, I'd missed that detail. I knew her favorite word for clemency. It was easy enough. But her ability to control shadows? That was something no one had ever spoken of.

As she caressed her palm with the end of the heart-shaped crop and one of those shadows stroked my cheek, I realized I did not mind the surprise. It was an interesting sensation, to be bound by something not corporeal. It was heavy and weightless all at once—tendrils of smoke with the ability to harden into ropes. What else she could do with them made me curious, especially with how she was staring at me right then.

Hunger burned in her scarlet eyes, her lips twitching in delighted satisfaction. She dragged the crop across her hand again, and my chest caved with a heavy exhale. Her heels were light on the floor, clopping and stalking as she made her way toward me. And when she reached me, she moved the crop slowly up the center of my chest, from my abs up between my pectorals—a steady progression that caused my cock to twitch with anticipation. She stepped around the chair, letting that leather tease my body with every excruciating second.

The first strike across my pec elicited a gasp from within me. Her lips flinched upward, the two different colors of her eyes staring me down with delighted glory. She struck again, harder this time. My skin tingled beneath the red sting, but every strike made my cock strain.

"You like this, don't you," she asked, that dark velvet voice so like a torturous song that my eyes rolled. Her nails raked across the back of my neck as the crop once more tickled my chest.

She brought it down again—grasping my hair and pulling my head back as she did, and I shifted in my seat as precum dribbled over the length of my dick. Her deep chuckle vibrated the thick air.

"You do," she taunted. Her fingers ran through my hair, rough and demeaning, yet the most delicious head massage I'd ever experienced. She leaned over me, her breasts brushing the back of my head.

"I'm going to suck your cock, hunter," she whispered against my lips. "And every time you think about coming, I'll remind you to who you belong to tonight."

Her teeth grabbed onto my bottom lip, and tugging until blood sprang from my flesh. The kiss she pressed to my cheek made me attempt to lean up, but to no avail, and I was left struggling against the chair as she came back around to my front.

"I love this," she said, tracing the heart-shaped mark she'd left on the right side of my chest. "How many of these will you have before this night is over? Will you listen to your mistress, or will you behave poorly enough for me to mark up all these beautiful muscles?"

I didn't respond, too caught up in the way her hips moved, how she was taunting me with her every breath. And fucking hell, when she crouched to her knees and spread my knees wide, I sank my head back onto the armchair and swallowed.

Her warm tongue cut the cold air surrounding us as she licked up the length of my dick, and then she wrapped her lips around the tip.

I'd thought her work was demonic magic before. But seeing her so in control was a drug. The relief of needing to control what was happening washed over me with each move of her mouth down my dick. My hands strained to touch her.

"Mm…"

"Mary—"

The crop struck my bicep this time, making my muscle flinch.

"You taste too good to finish already, hunter," she said, stilling her tongue on my tip. I groaned at the sight of watching her dangle that tongue, at the pink raise of my skin. I stifled that need to release, forcing myself to relax as she pinched my balls, and my cock disappeared inside her mouth again.

Fuck, I wasn't sure how long I would last with the way she gagged, how she hummed that sweet little lullaby around me... Gods, she was torture and pleasure. The tingles on my pricked skin had me squirming against her shadows, but they weren't letting up at all. She had me puddling in her hands, her mouth, her ecstasy. I dug my nails so tightly into the armchair that I left behind streaks. I didn't know how much longer I could last.

Mary straightened, slurping on her spit as she pushed her breasts around my dick and rose her shoulders, giving me an innocent smile.

"Good little hunter," she cooed. "You're doing so well. Shall I let you come down my throat? Or would you like to come across my chest?"

Her hand squeezed my tip with her words. I sucked in a sharp breath and simply stared at her, knowing the choice was hers. But I spoke anyway.

"Throat," I said. "I want to see my cum on your tongue. *Please*," I added.

She pouted, her dark lips puckering like she'd been waiting on that word. "How can I possibly deny such words?" Her grin spread wide. "Very well. Choke me one more time, hunter. Coat my throat with your cum."

I tried to move my hips, but she scratched her nails across my abs. My cock hit the back of her throat, then further, deep-throating me until there was no more left to see. She set an excruciating pace that made me shift, made me call out her name, and curse the world. I fell into the deep end, breaths growing faster and faster with her every suck and slurp. There was no stopping my release this time. I wasn't in control of this. I was lost beneath the feel of her swirling tongue and sucking lips.

She dragged her teeth along the topside of my dick, and I lost everything. I spilled and spilled down her throat. I'd never come so hard for anyone before. The groans that left me were not of my own. She possessed my body, my mind. And as she stilled with my cock down her throat, swallowing nearly all of what I had in me, I collapsed into the seat.

When her warm tongue disappeared from my spent cock, I finally opened my eyes again. She rose over me, and I could see my cum on her tongue when she opened her mouth, that sadistic smile wide on her licentious lips. She curled her tongue in a U-shape and paused over me, and as the milky substance dripped down that path, I couldn't stop myself from sticking out my own tongue and catching the drop that fell from her mouth.

Break The Glass

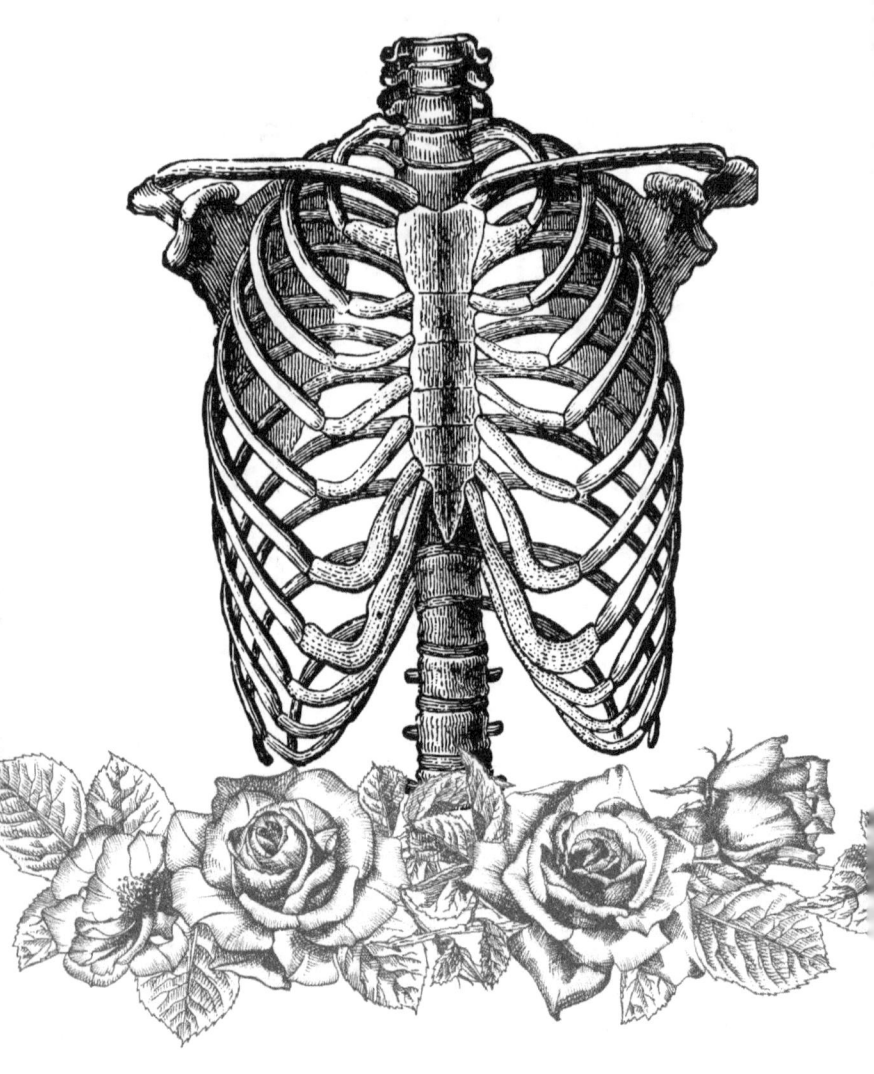

Chapter Seven
Mary

DAMON'S surrender was more delicious than any mortal I'd played with in the past.

That *sweet, sweet* surrender... I wanted to bathe in it.

I pulled his button-down shirt over my shoulders and crawled onto the back of the armchair, sitting my ass on the top, my legs spread wide on either side of him, and I slowly began to massage his shoulders.

His head rolled with a groan, and I smiled at the red marks across his torso, watching him continue to come down from what I'd just put him through.

"Fucking hell, demon... What are you doing?" he asked.

"Good boys get rewards," I said.

He tilted his head back and looked up at me. "Remove your shadows," he said.

I considered him, my fingers digging hard into

his collar. "What will you do if I take them off?"

"Touch you," he said.

I didn't reply, and instead pulled on his chin to make him look straight into my mirror again, to stare at his marked flesh and my spread cunt so close to his tongue. His shoulders caved as I moved my hands down his chest, taking care around the heart-shaped welted marks on his skin. And when I was done massaging him, I pushed off the chair and strode over to the desk.

A glass of whiskey appeared in my hand, and I took a sip as I loosened his restraints. The shadows melted around his arms, his ankles, and when he realized he was free, Damon stood and rubbed his wrists.

His slow prowl had me on alert as he made his way across the room to me. Shadows trailed in his wake, daring him to try anything—

He launched with the last few feet, and I sent bindings around his throat, holding him in place not three inches away. Rage and desire shone in his eyes, but the hold didn't deter him. He reached out, his fingers delicately roaming over my exposed sternum, the pads highlighting the scar as he traced it.

"I should kill you right here, demon," he hissed. "I should flay you for what you just did."

My eyes fluttered as he leaned closer, his hand

cupping my breast. "Flay me," I whispered into his ear, letting his restraints slacken. "Cut my skin with iron. Burn my body with that necklace in your pocket." My teeth caught his earlobe and tugged, and his grip tightened.

"End me."

"You're everything I mean to be rid of in this world," he said as his hand on my hip moved to my thigh. "Everything I've devoted my career to hunting down."

My bottom lip sagged as he drew close enough that I could feel his breath on my lips. I opened my mouth to speak, but his fingers thrust between my thighs, the other beneath my chin. My lips curled with an audible hiss, nails digging into the lip of the wood desk at my back.

"And yet..." He pulled back enough to lock our eyes, and a triumphant smile lifted the corners of my mouth at the surrender and absolute desire in his darkened gaze.

"And yet, the thought of not tasting you right now makes me want to end myself."

He pulled me into him by the neck, his lips slamming into mine. Harshly, like every twist and wrench of our tongues together might kill the other. I bit his lip until the coppery tang of blood wet my taste buds. Damon's kiss was feral and full of the hatred and loathing I knew he felt for me.

His fingers twisted into my hair as he moved to my throat—biting and licking, his fingers clawing at my flesh. Every dig of his ravenous touch had me growing wetter and wetter for him to be inside me.

He picked me up onto the desk, his hands spreading my knees wide. I leaned back, letting him suck and bite on my nipples, and just when his ravenous acts grew too hungry, I moved up my leg and slammed my high heel into his chest.

Damon winced before straightening and pulling his hands off of me.

"Greedy boy," I taunted. "Hasn't anyone ever taught you manners?"

A low grunt sounded from within him. "I have manners," he said.

"Then I expect you know to pray before you feast," I replied. My head lifted, and I nodded toward the ground. "On your knees."

Damon's jaw clenched, angered that I'd starved him a few minutes longer, but he knelt, one knee dropping, followed by the other, and I sat up and pushed my ass to the edge of the desk. His tongue darted out over his lips as he stared at my gleaming pussy, so anxious and ready for him to taste.

He reached for my calf and began to unzip my boot. "Heavenly gods…" the boot slid off my leg as smooth as his voice. Chills ran over my skin with every word he said, every touch he graced me with. "Bless me, for I have sinned," he said, moving to my other leg. "Forgive me, for the night is dark, the light is gone, and she is the scarlet glow leading me to dawn." His lips landed on the inside of my knee, prompting my back to arch as he made his way up, my smile shining at the ceiling.

He lifted my thighs over his shoulders, kissing my inner thigh. His breath blew across my clit, making me suck in a sharp breath. "Let my tongue lead her to salvation—" His first lick made me flinch "—let her taste feed my greed—" His tongue stroked my entire pussy before circling my clit again "—for I am just a hungry boy, knelt before a goddess." He sucked my clit into his mouth, making me moan.

"Bless me to do as she wishes," he breathed. "Bless this night… Bless this feast… *Amen*."

Bless this fucking man.

I nearly fell back onto the table as he laid into me. His fingers dug into my hips, creasing my flesh and bruising my pale skin. Every starved lick and stroke of his tongue had me moaning his name and nearly screaming. I braced my bent knees around his shoulders, pinning him in place, and every time I looked down, my stomach fluttered with the desire in his gaze.

As his tongue darted in and out of my entrance, I tried to deny the orgasm rising in my every muscle. My toes curled as I clawed at the desk, leaving behind indentions in the wood. His short nails delved so deeply into me that he broke my skin. I flinched with the pleasing pain and wiggled against his tease.

I could hardly hold myself together, much less hold off my orgasm. I wanted to. I didn't want his torture to end. I needed this release, this level of devotion… my body craved what he gave me, and as I reached my end, I knew he craved me too.

Damon slid two fingers inside me, cursed, and sucked my clit into his mouth before whispering, "You're so tight for me, demon. Are you going to come on my tongue?"

I glanced down between my thighs. "Is that what you want?" I asked. "Do you want to taste my cum?"

He removed his fingers and replaced them with his tongue, muttering a quick, "Yes."

I ran my hands through his soft hair and leaned down to give him a lingering kiss. He sucked his lips around my tongue, letting me taste myself, and I stroked his cheek when I pulled back.

"Make me come, hunter," I said.

My back hit the desk again when he pursed his lips around my clit again and plunged his fingers inside me. He worked with unrelenting indulgence, intent on sending me over the edge. And damn, if he did. My body began to convulse. I couldn't breathe. Every muscle within me writhed to the very end of my rope. I couldn't hold it in.

I came with a scream, my hips rocking against his mouth as I grabbed the edge of the table. Damon licked me until he was back on his feet, holding my thighs and ass against his chest. And when he was satisfied that I had been depleted, he let me back down onto the desk's surface.

My chest continued to heave as he released me, but one look at how hard his cock was once again sent me spinning. I grabbed and pulled his lips to mine.

Every inch of his torso lined up against me, his cock nudging at my sensitive wetness. I bit his lip, drawing blood to the surface again as his hands entangled in my hair. I needed his dick inside me, needed him to fuck me rough and dirty.

As he moved to bite my neck, I caught a glimpse of the crescent blood marks on my thighs from his nails, the bruises his hands had already left there. He yanked my hair to expose my neck further and pulled my breast from beneath the lingerie with the other hand. I gasped with the pleasure of his teeth on my peaked nipple, his harsh touch making me spiral.

I reached between us, grasping his cock with both hands and squeezing as I stroked him. Air hissed between his teeth when he pulled back to look at me, and I gave him a smirk.

"Fuck me like you hate me, hunter," I dared. "Give me what's mine."

Damon shoved me backward, his hand pressing my face into the desk, thrusting inside me. Both of us cursed, and for a few seconds, Damon didn't move. He paused like he was adjusting himself, letting me adjust to him. My pussy ached with the stretch and fill. Damn him for feeling so delicious. I rocked my hips up to meet his, letting him in deeper, and he pulled out—nearly to the tip—before pounding back inside me. Again. Again. And again. Each time with more power than the last.

"Yes," I called out as his fingers hooked onto my hips. His pace picked up, though the savageness of his thrusts did not dwindle. Sweat beaded on his forehead. His face twisted as he held himself on the edge.

I clawed my way up his chest, making sure to scratch open his skin as I did, and I kissed him hard. Teeth clashed, our tongues battling for dominance. He slapped my ass, causing me to pull up on his shoulders and moan into his mouth.

"That's right," I said. "*Harder*."

He spanked me again, his calloused hands raking over my bare flesh. I reached for his face, squeezing his cheeks between my fingers again.

"Harder," I breathed. "Make me see stars."

I wanted him to rip me in half.

His hand slammed down on my sternum and held me against the table as he fucked me, just like I wanted. Rough and savage and downright unforgiving—as if he meant to crack my chest and pelvis with his moves. I screamed, unable to control myself, and with my scream, the mansion shuddered, the candles flickered, and my mirror trembled.

"Right there—*Fuck, yes, hunter*—" I grabbed the lip of the desk behind me as my back arched off the wood, my end at that edge.

"Shit, Mary—I'm—"

I came around his cock, and he spilled inside me just after. Breath escaped me as it did him, and Damon collapsed against my chest.

Our sweat mingled when he lay atop me. I ran my fingers through his hair, pushing the damp strands back. My mouth was dry and sticky with saliva, but I managed to speak softly.

"Take us to the armchair," I requested.

Damon straightened and inhaled deeply. He pulled from within me, his cum dripping from my pussy. For a moment, he simply stared. I knew I was red, swollen, and bruised from his fucking, and I loved the way he looked at what he'd done to me.

I dragged my finger delicately down his cheek, prompting him to look at me. "You did so well, my love," I said. "*So, so* well."

Chapter Eight
Mary

DAMON moved us to the armchair, where I sat on his lap and hummed a song as I traced the scars on his chest, occasionally pushing his hair back or kissing his neck. There were a few scars on his chest that intrigued me, the ones that were rounder and indented rather than raised.

"Tell me about these," I said as I rubbed over one.

"Why?" he said, breaking out of his daze.

"I'm curious," I replied, and he cocked a brow at me. My mouth curled at the right corner, remembering our earlier conversation.

"Tell me about yours," he said. "I'll tell you about mine."

"I like bargains," I said with a shrug as I drew a line down his cheek. "The stories about me are all true. All the blood they say is on my hands is real. I've tortured so many that I've lost count... but I still remember their screams. Most of my scars came before I was killed."

"How?" he asked.

I didn't respond at first. The memories of those days before I took matters into my own hands poured through me and chilled my insides. But a bargain was a bargain.

"My father had a fondness for the whip," I admitted. "While my younger brothers were out doing whatever they pleased, I was stuck inside being told how to serve wine and treated like some trophied prize to marry off. But each scar he put on me tainted and broke me for every man who came along. Eventually, he gave up. And when he died, while I thought I was free of his tyranny, I was wrong. My brothers, no matter how much younger they were than I, thought they, too, deserved the right to strike me." I paused to look at Damon, considering the way he looked at me then. "In the end, they screamed for me just like they always told me I would for them."

"And this one?" Damon asked, running a finger over my cheek.

"After death," I said. "The first demon hunter to nearly catch me. He sent his hounds after me. One was quite the jumper."

Damon's fingers rubbed and squeezed my ass gently as we sat there. I could see his mind working behind his eyes, see the questions he begged to ask me.

"The necklace... what's the story there?" he asked.

"You're so nosy," I teased.

"I want to know why I had to search so hard for the damned thing."

I glanced down at where I knew the necklace lay in his pants on the floor. "A damned thing it is," I agreed. "The only man I ever loved gave me that. My father killed him when he found out. He wasn't good enough for Father's standards."

Damon's jaw clenched, his hand squeezing my thigh, but he didn't push the subject. "The family that lived here," he began. "You didn't take the children."

"Children are innocent," I replied. "Now, their parents... Their father was fun before I took his heart. The mother... she begged so nicely for her children to be spared. Even when I assured her they would be, she continued to sob. Sobbing can be such a bore. At least the father played along."

Damon reached out to my pouting lips and gave my chin a flick. "Only a demon would call a mother's last pleas for her children's lives a 'bore,'" he said.

I shifted in his lap and licked his ear again. "A bargain, hunter," I said. "I believe you owe me your own story. Are your scars from previous hunts?"

He sighed a deep sigh that I knew all too well, his eyes avoiding mine. "Those three scars are from gunshots," he said. "Exit wounds."

"Someone tried to kill me with those a few years ago." I said. "Scared little idiot. Ran right into my mirror when I chased him." I traced a finger down Damon's chest, over a few of the other scars on his abs.

"What about these?" I asked.

"Ah… my brothers," he admitted, and I perked up in his lap.

"Someone you care about harmed you?" I asked.

"We were kids," he said. "We didn't know any better."

A lie, I knew. Though, I wasn't sure I was getting the whole of his story right then. Perhaps because he didn't trust me, or he simply didn't find it necessary to tell me. I leaned into him and gave his cheek a lingering kiss.

"Break my mirror, and no one is ever harming you again," I swore.

A low chuckle came from him. "You think I need you to protect me, demon?"

"I think you'd like someone to protect you for once," I replied.

His eyes flickered to mine for a brief moment

before he moved closer. Our noses grazed, and I held his shoulders a little tighter.

"Sounds like you're trying to work some sort of actual bargain," he said.

"Or maybe I know you're reluctant to slice my throat after tonight," I said.

"Someone thinks very highly of her cunt," he taunted.

My lips twitched as our faces drew even closer. "I feel the way you respond to me," I whispered. "I know you've never responded to anyone this way. I know the only way you'll ever be satisfied is with the threat of the chase and adrenaline pouring through your veins. You were made for a demon, hunter... And my pussy is the one your cock chose."

His lips swallowed mine into a kiss fueled by the hate that I was right. He grasped me beneath my ass and squeezed harshly as he took to his feet. I could feel his greed in the way he moved his tongue, the way he grabbed me, the way his cock hardened just from our bodies flush.

One knee on the floor, followed by the other. My back hit the broken circle as he laid me down, and with one swift move of my fingers, every candle in the room and on the floor lit. Light from the red stick candles illuminated our bodies. My nails dragged down his back, marking and drawing blood from beneath his skin. He sucked in a sharp breath, his teeth clamping down on my nipple as he grabbed my thigh and pulled it high around his ribs.

Every lick and bite caused my back to arch off the floor. We were scrambling for each other, feral for the touch of the other. Wild and sadistic and hungry for every kiss and bite and draw of blood. He rocked against me as we made out, his dick hardening quickly. I was soaking from the need in his kiss and grasp. No other man had ever taken to pleasuring me like this—confident in his movements, assertive in his lips... He was a conquest worth being aroused for, and with sunrise approaching, I took the time to savor him.

I rolled us over and pushed his chest into the floor, digging my nails into his chest as I sank onto his erected length. "Your cock was made to fuck me, hunter," I said as his skin welted beneath my fingers. "Your tongue was meant for my cunt..." I bent over him, his fingers digging into my generous ass, and I kissed him slowly. My clit dragged over his pelvis as I moved, sparking that delicious warmth in the pit of my stomach. His eyes glazed over with every slow movement, chest arching off the floor when he cursed.

"I am the demon your body craves, the goddess of your nightmares, the chase your mind desires. I am the darkest want of your little black heart. No other can compare to this, to what I can do to you…"

Shadows crawled around us, sweeping over his chest and neck, licking at his balls and his ass. His eyes widened at the sensation, and I pushed his chest back onto the floor.

"Fuck, Mary—"

"Shh…" I whispered, placing a finger upon his lips. "Relax, my love… Bend your knees for me. Let me in."

Damon hesitated as he stared at me, obviously wary of what I offered. I smiled at his pause and gave him a lingering kiss.

"You're adorable," I cooed. "Remember your word, hunter," I said as the shadows swirled. I leaned over him and licked up his face, eliciting a curse from his lips. "Beg when you've had enough."

My shadows slid into his ass, taking it slowly and mimicking a single finger and another massaging his balls. And as I felt what they did, chills erupted over my flesh. He groaned so nicely with every stroke, relaxing bit by bit as he let me in.

I started at a slow pace and worked up with every grind of his hips and sharp inhale of his breath. His cock twitched inside me, every vein in his neck rising with the strain of trying to deny himself release.

"Fucking—*Mary*—I'm going to—"

No. No, not yet.

I grabbed his face, puckering his mouth again. "Don't you fucking dare," I hissed.

Shadows evacuated from around us. A low growl sounded in his throat. I bared my teeth, gripping his face tighter.

"You're *mine*," I swore. "You come when I tell you to. You breathe when I tell you to. You fuck me *like* I tell you to." I shoved his face into the floor and raised my chin. "Say it, hunter."

I released his face and straightened over him. He glowered as he rolled his head and locked eyes with me. "I'm yours," he rasped.

My hands dragged up his chest and I leaned down to kiss him again—a gesture he returned as his fingers squeezed my hips.

"Good boy," I said. I gave his cheek a harsh pat and smeared the blood across his face from where I'd grabbed him. "Now, turn me over and fuck me like you hate everything I've done to you tonight. Fuck me dirty and hard and without restraint. I don't want to feel my body when we're done."

Fire flared in his eyes as his fingers dug so deep into my ass that I gasped, and I smiled at his obedience when he slapped my bare skin.

"On your hands and knees then, woman," he

growled.

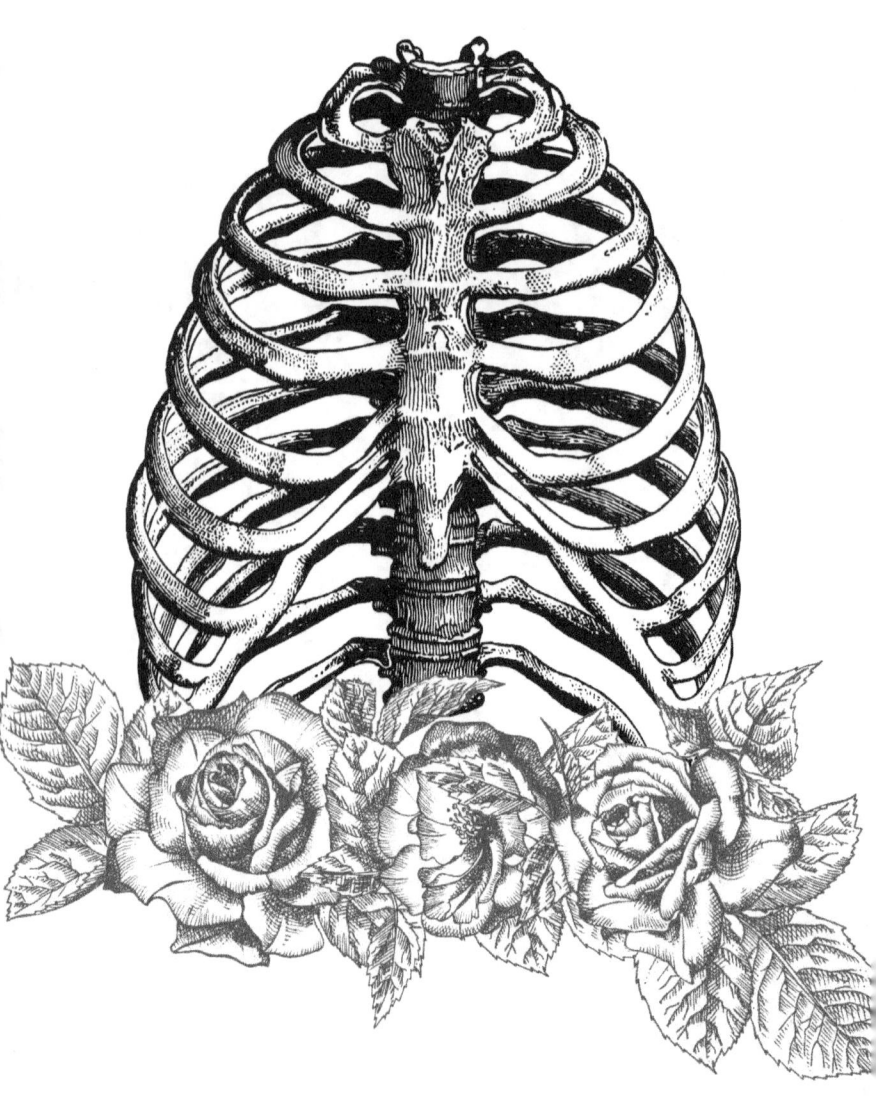

Chapter Nine
Damon

SHE was right.

She was everything I didn't know I would crave. And the way her shadows moved around and inside me? Again, something I didn't know I wanted. But fucking hell, I did.

Only her. She was the only one I'd get on my knees for, the only one I'd let fuck me until I couldn't remember my name, until amnesia flooded my mind and all I could remember was her.

Scarlet fucking Mary.

She moved from atop me, and I swung her beneath me to her stomach, pressing her head into the floor. Her laughter rippled over the air and made the candlelight flicker. I pushed her knees up, making her bend, her back arch, and she flattened her hands onto the ground. Her ass wiggled before me, spread wide and awaiting, her pussy glistening. I raked a hand over her broad hip before spanking her flesh. A moan elicited from inside her as I watched her skin rise pink.

"That's right, demon," I said as I sank two fingers inside her awaiting cunt.

She flinched with every strike of my palm against her, every thrust of my fingers in her pussy —until her skin pricked scarlet, and she whimpered for me.

I cursed under my breath and kissed her spine. Precum dripped from my dick in anticipation of being inside her again. I stroked myself as she moved her hips, wriggling and teasing me with the sight. I caught her amused gaze in the mirror and wondered what exactly she was planning in her devious mind.

But as her shadows trickled around us, I began to have an idea.

"Give me that cock, Damon," she said. "Fuck my pussy until I'm destroyed."

I obliged.

I grabbed her hair and threw her head back at the same time that my dick slammed inside her. Fuck, I wondered if she was using some sort of possessive powers on me. I couldn't get enough of this, of her.

"Look at us," she whispered from her knees as one of the shadows dragged beneath my chin—a finger commanding attention.

The grip of her drenching pussy, the feel of her resistance as I pulled her hair and grabbed her hip, the shadow at my back... I knew where this was going, and as another shadow tickled my balls, my ass, I yanked her head back until she was forced to stare at the ceiling, and I relaxed for her.

The cool umbra filled me as I filled her, and I released a singing hiss of surrender at the sensation. I could have stopped her at any moment, thrown her back into the mirror she wanted me to look into or killed her with the fire poker within my reach. But fucking hell... this had me on an edge I couldn't help but ride.

One glance in the mirror nearly undid me. Her mouth was open, her body moving with every deepened thrust of my cock inside her, breasts bouncing, the red scratches on her chest and the bright pink of her spanked ass, the shadows curled all around us—including the one sliding slowly in and out of me.

Her devious chuckle filled my ears as she pulled the hand I had on her hip to between her thighs.

"You like my shadows, hunter?" she cooed. "You like the way they fill you up, don't you?"

My thumb rolled over her clit before I pinched it between my fingers. She gasped and groaned at the sensation, her fist rocking into the floor, and the shadow behind me pulled out and slammed inside me. I cried out, thrusting harder into her as I fought release. My balls tightened with her torture, and another shadow came to tickle my sensitive skin.

Those shadowed fingers curled around my chin and pulled my head toward it—a duplicate silhouette of Mary hugged my back. This was the creature filling me, torturing me. Its coolness swarmed my mouth, a shadowed tongue slipping inside my mouth. My cock twitched inside Mary, and the shadow shoved me forward. Mary was smiling again. I wondered if she could feel what her shadow was doing to me.

"Fuck, Mary," I moaned with every thrust of the other and her pussy tightening. I was at the precipice of release, teetering on the very edge.

"Mary, I need to—"

Her shadow licked my face and turned my head toward the mirror again. Mary pushed off her hands and arched so that I could hold my hands on her bouncing breasts.

"Almost, hunter," she moaned. "Fuck, right there. *Yes.*"

Her face scrunched as I pinched her nipples, desperate to feel her come around me as she'd done before. I needed this before I lost control.

A few more thrusts and every muscle in me strained. Sweat beaded off my forehead. The veins in my arms nearly cracked out of my skin.

Mary came with a scream, and I wholly subdued inside her. I spilled over, emptying myself inside her wicked cunt. Her shadow slipped out of me. I slumped over her, my body giving out, and once more, Mary laughed.

"Mine," she cooed, her hand running through my hair. "Go ahead, hunter. Say you'll keep me."

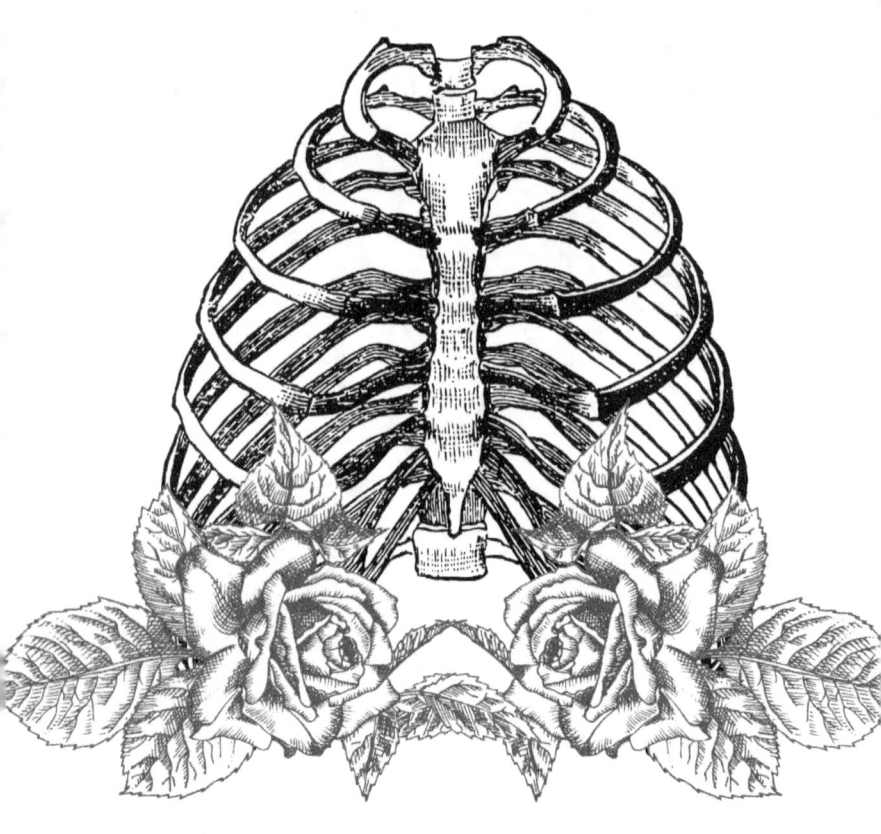

Chapter Ten
Damon

It took me a few moments to realize what she'd said.

I could see the night lightening through the bay window behind her mirror and knew we didn't have long. Turmoil rattled my stomach as I pulled out of her arms and stood to put my pants on.

Keep her.

I couldn't. No matter how she'd made me feel, I could never keep her.

I saw her stand out the corner of my eye as I buckled my pants. My movements slowed as I watched her, waiting on her to make her move to either kill me or try to run. But she didn't have much time with the sun being so close to the horizon.

"What will it be, hunter?" she asked.

Candlelight flickered off something in her hand. I reacted before she had a chance.

I twisted, pulling my knife from my pocket, and I launched in her direction just as she lunged toward me. A struggle ensued. She writhed in my grasp, her nails turning into talons. They scratched my skin open, making me cry out, but I threw her across the desk and thrust my knife to her throat.

"Give me a reason not to be rid of you for good," I said in a strained voice.

A grin appeared on her lips. "Because you're having too much fun," she said, those differently shaded carmine eyes pouring through me. "You want this... you want *me*, and you want me too much to kill me." She leaned in, her tongue licking my ear as she whispered, "Break the glass. I'll be your good little pet during the day, but at night, you'll be mine."

Her nails scratched down my throat, raising my skin beneath the red welt.

"The moment I set you free, you'll run away or kill me," I said.

"I could kill you now if I wanted," she affirmed. "But why would I when I could watch you chase after me instead. Again and again and again."

I didn't realize I was shaking until I saw black blood trickling from her neck. I shoved her and straightened, taking three steps back from her poisonous body. Mary sat up and pushed off the desk, her hips swaying as she came toward me.

"We could be partners, you and I," she said. "Imagine the fun we could have together. Chasing demons and horrible people. We could toy with them, fuck over their dead bodies once we've rid the world of their terror."

"Unleashing you upon the world would be terror enough," I countered.

"I'll behave," she said, a smile lifting her dark lips. She paused just before me and lifted her chin smugly. "Break the glass, Damon," she said as she looked to her left.

I followed her gaze to the mirror, and Mary moved behind me, her head poking around my shoulder, her arms curling around my chest. Shadowed hands draped over me. I couldn't turn away from our reflections—the power and devastation in us together, both covered in scars left behind from pasts we'd run from.

We were the same, she and I.

And I was devastated for her.

For her tease, her taste, her curves. Fire reflected off her poison red hair as she stepped past the circle's line and toward her mirror. Something tugged at my gut. Something that told me not to let her go. Probably just my cock being greedy for the feel of her again, but…

"What did you do to me, demon?" I snapped.

Mary stood up on her toes and bit the lobe of my

ear. "Shown you your darkest desire," came her venomous whisper. "What will it be, my love?"

I didn't answer.

My silence chilled the room. The candles flickered like a breeze had washed over them. I had only a few minutes to make that decision. Keep her, control her with the necklace I had, with the threat of death, and hope to hell that she didn't kill me. Or force her back in that mirror for another idiot to come along and set her free—one that might not know how to handle her, one that might be ignorant to her games.

Mary kissed my cheek and stepped in front of me. An almost sadness filled her gaze as she wrapped her hands against my face and then gave me a kiss, one that burned my lips after she let me go.

"Will you summon me again?" she asked as she moved backward toward the mirror, apparently having given up that I would set her free.

I hesitated.

I could. I could summon her anytime I wished. I could take the mirror with me. She would be mine to control and wield, once a year, a few hours at a time.

Or…

"Maybe," I answered.

Her lips quirked upward at the corner, but she

just turned on her heel.

With one last glance at me through the reflection, she blew a kiss, then stepped one foot inside the mirror, the glass rippling like water over the surface.

"Until next time, Damon," she said.

My heart dropped. Every muscle curled with anxiety as I watched her move in slow motion back into that prison. Sunlight dared to crack over the horizon. I couldn't breathe.

And for whatever reason, I grabbed the fire poker beside the armchair.

"Bargain with me," I said.

Mary paused. "What?"

"Swear you'll never run away from me or disappear, that you'll never kill me, and I'll set you free," I said.

She pulled her leg from inside the mirror, her eyes wide with surprise. "I swear."

"Swear on this." I pulled the necklace out, and Mary swallowed.

Mary nodded. "I swear on whatever is left of my existence, on my necklace."

The necklace glowed, and I knew the bargain had been made. I tossed the poker over in my hands and looked past her into the mirror again.

"Back up."

I wasn't entirely sure about what I was about to

do, but I knew the moment I picked up the poker that it was the right thing. A demon hunter with a demon for his partner, his lover... It was crazy. Insane. What kind of person would unleash such a beast unto this world again?

I would.

Glass shattered as the sun broke. The mansion shuddered. The candles blew out. And I kept swinging. I destroyed that mirror; I destroyed the curse.

Mary was free.

Epilogue
Damon

THE black '67 Chevelle glimmered in the sunlight outside a mansion in upstate New York. I pulled my gloves up, stretching my fingers one at a time as I peered to a third-story window, and caught a shadow passing by.

We'd been hunting this one for nearly a year now. The spirit was rampant and loved to haunt teens on the railroad tracks that crossed over the property. We'd tested the story the night before—to drive over the tracks and sit idle. A lantern had appeared after a few minutes of sitting there, along with the sound of a train engine. It grew louder and louder, like the train was coming our way, but the tracks had been dead for centuries. The light moved closer, more prominent. Someone ran past the car, and the train blew straight through us.

We'd laughed and fucked in the backseat after, adrenaline scorching through us.

Because we'd sat through the ordeal, the running spirit did not chase us; now, it was our turn to chase it.

I opened the passenger door. Mary's hair blazed so brightly, it reminded me of fire. It always reminded me of fire. She reached for my hand as she stepped out of the car, her high heels unsteady on the gravelly driveway. But Mary didn't falter.

She'd behaved as well as expected over the last year. I'd kept her close, and she'd kept her end of the bargain, only running when we played after a kill.

Mary reached out and wiped the lipstick off my jaw—the lipstick she'd just planted there after she'd sucked my dick on the drive over.

"Plum is your color," she said with a smirk. "It looks so pretty around your cock too." Her gaze lifted to the mansion behind us, and she whipped off her cat-eye sunglasses. "Who are we here to kill again?"

"Eager to kill your own kind?" I asked.

"Eager to play," she replied.

I closed the trunk of the car, not bothering to hand her a weapon. *She* was the weapon. She was the bait, the nightmare, the ventriloquist. Each time another demon saw her, they either ran or laughed like they thought I was the one in trouble.

Things were much more fun with her around.

My demon. My woman. My Mary.

Mary. Mary. Mary.

THANK YOU
for reading

Break the Glass
A Halloween erotica novella

If you enjoyed this story, please consider leaving a review on Amazon, Goodreads, social media sites, or your preferred review site. Reviews really mean a lot (even if it is just a couple lines) and help us as authors get our stories out there.

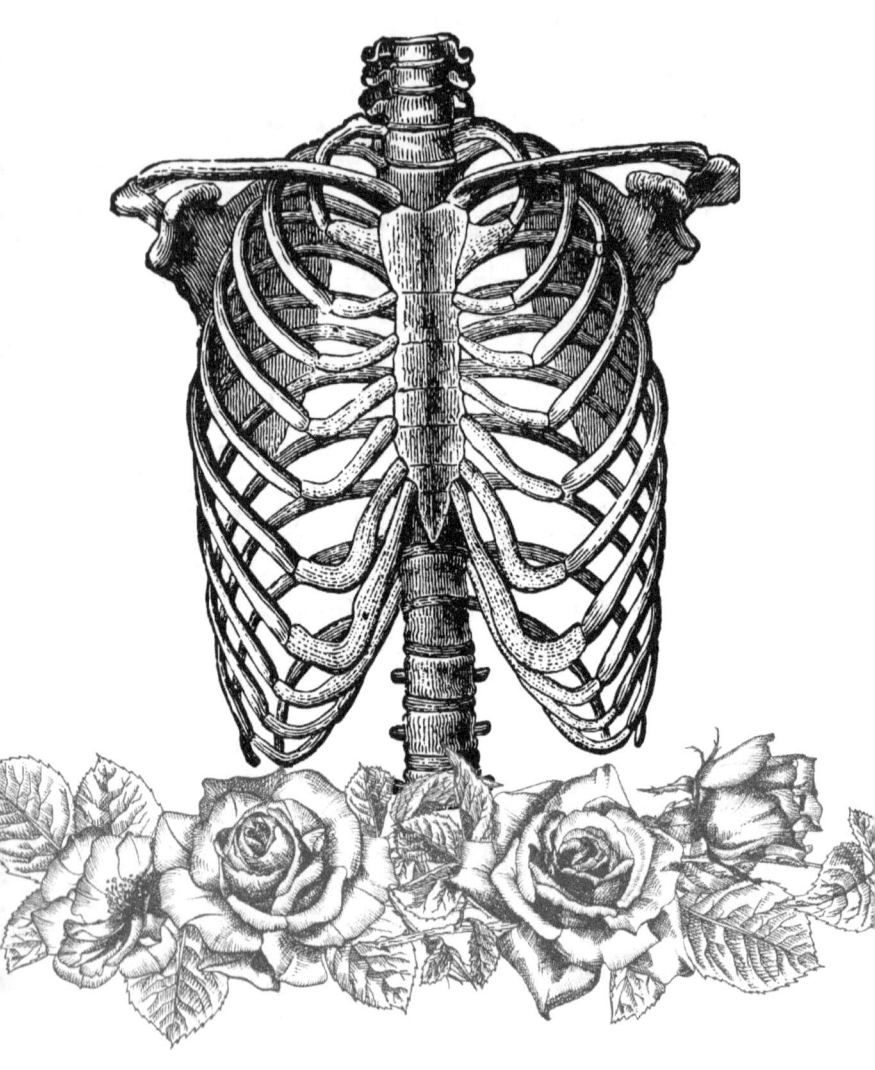

Acknowledgements

THIS fall has been an absolute rollercoaster of not knowing whether this one was going to make it out in time and getting ready for my first child to be born, on top of a slew of other things that would take up this entire page to name!

I want to thank all of you so much for being patient and sticking with me through all of this. It truly means so much that you continue to support and read my works! I'm going to keep this one short (yes, actually short this time!)

Thank you to my amazing street team, Kay, Alexis, Leighann, Angie (you are amazing), Emily, Ashley, Pru, all the ARC readers, those making endless posts and tiktoks including my works, ALL the readers, and most importantly, my family.

I would not be where I am without all of you and it would be impossible to thank you enough for everything you do.

Next year, I'll be focusing back in on my established series books, and I can't wait to revisit those characters and worlds. I miss my Haerland (Honest Scrolls series) characters, my Sam and Ana, and my Gavin and Chloe.

Thank you all for sticking with me and being the best group of readers I could ask for.

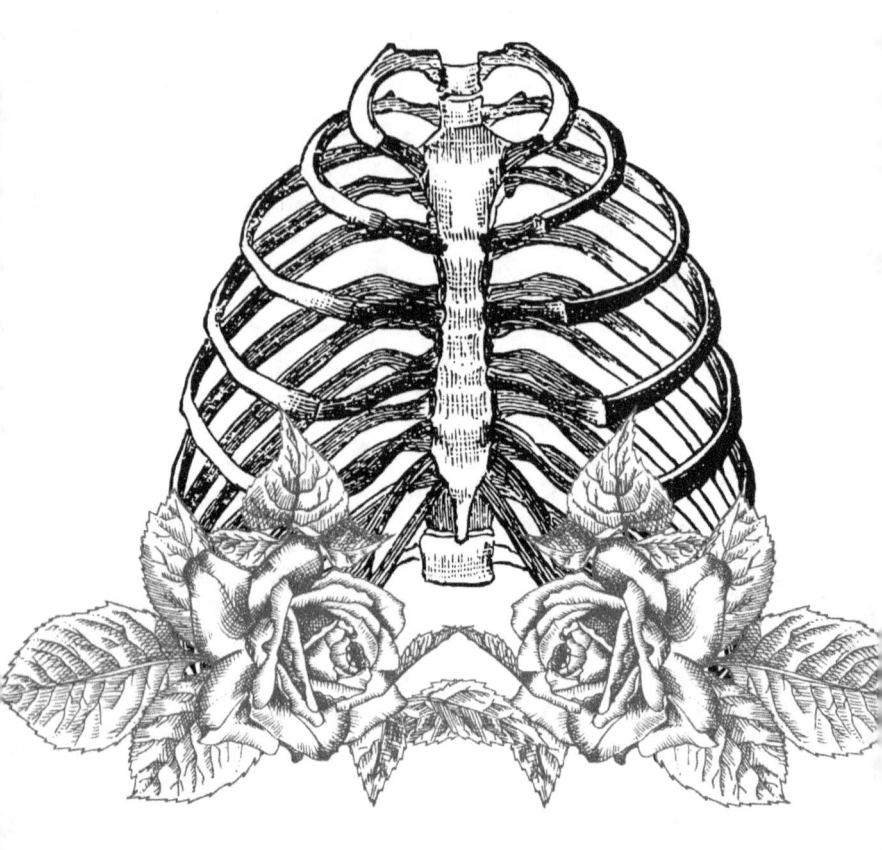

Other Works

Now Available:

Dead Moons Rising
Book One in the Honest Scrolls Series

Flames of Promise
Book Two in the Honest Scrolls Series

The Gathering
An Honest Scrolls Novella

Sweet Girl
A Cupid Novella

Ballad of Nightmares
Book one in the Nightmares Duology

Anyone And You
An autumn erotica novella

Break The Glass
A Halloween erotica Novella

Coming Soon in 2023:

Finding You
A Sweet Girl Novel
April 2023

About the Author

Jack Whitney is an adult dark fantasy and romance author out of North Carolina, US.

You can usually find her playing in dark and strange worlds. Her characters are always in charge.
She is fueled by coffee, whiskey, and shadow daydreams.
If you're reading her books, they probably came with a warning label.

Welcome to the Nightmare of Ravens.

Jack also feels very weird about writing bios because she's not sure what you want to know. She is almost always stalking social media and procrastinating, so if you would like to find her to ask more questions, please feel free.

@Jack.Whitney.Writer

www.ingramcontent.com/pod-product-compliance
Lightning Source LLC
Chambersburg PA
CBHW060335260626
47160CB00007B/2803